APR   2019

# MIAMI
# MARLINS
## STARS, STATS, HISTORY, AND MORE!

BY K. C. KELLEY

**The Child's World®**
childsworld.com

Published by The Child's World®
1980 Lookout Drive • Mankato, MN 56003-1705
800-599-READ • www.childsworld.com

ISBN 9781503828285
LCCN 2018944842

Printed in the United States of America
PAO2392

Photo Credits:
Cover: Joe Robbins (2).
Inside: AP Images: Kyodo 5, Hans Deryk 17, Michael
Perez 19; Dreamstime.com: Jerry Coli 23; Newscom:
Roberto Koltun/TNS 13, Susan Knowles/UPI 20,
Rich von Bilberstein/Icon SMI 27, Juan Salas Icon SW 29;
Joe Robbins: 6, 9, 10, 14, 24.

## About the Author

K.C. Kelley is a huge sports
fan who has written more
than 100 books for kids. His
favorite sport is baseball.
He has also written about
football, basketball, soccer,
and even auto racing! He lives
in Santa Barbara, California.

## On the Cover

Main photo: Catcher J.T. Realmuto
Inset: former shortstop
Hanley Ramirez

# CONTENTS

# GO, MARLINS!

T alk about fast starts! The Miami Marlins were only four years old when they won their first **World Series** in 1997! They won again in 2003, but have struggled since then. Today's Marlins have a new owner with a championship past. Derek Jeter won four World Series and had 3,465 hits with the New York Yankees. As the Marlins owner, Jeter is trying to make the team winners again. Let's meet this great young ball club.

*Superstar Derek Jeter has left the field, but he stayed* ➤
*in baseball. He now runs the Marlins.*

# WHO ARE THE MARLINS?

The Marlins play in the National League (NL). That group is part of Major League Baseball (MLB). MLB also includes the American League (AL). There are 30 teams in MLB. The winner of the NL plays the winner of the AL in the World Series. The Marlins made it to two World Series not long after they began playing. Recent seasons have been disappointing. Miami fans want to go back to the top!

◄ *Outfielder Brian Anderson could be a star for the Marlins.*

# WHERE THEY CAME FROM

**B**aseball has a long history in Florida. Teams have gone there for spring training since the 1910s. No team called Florida home in the regular season . . . until the Marlins. They joined the NL as an **expansion** team in 1993. Thanks to some great young players, they were World Series champs in 1997. That was the fastest that any new team had become the champions. They were called the Florida Marlins until 2012.

*Hanley Ramirez was the top NL rookie in 2006 and ➤ later made three All-Star Games with the Marlins.*

# WHO THEY PLAY

The Marlins play in the NL East Division. The other teams in the NL East are the Atlanta Braves, the New York Mets, the Philadelphia Phillies, and the Washington Nationals. The Marlins play more games against their division **rivals** than against other teams. In all, the Marlins play 162 games each season. They play 81 games at home and 81 on the road.

◄ *Infielder Starlin Castro could help the Marlins get back to the top.*

# WHERE THEY PLAY

**M**arlins Park opened for the 2012 season. It is the third-smallest stadium in MLB, with room for just over 37,000 fans inside. Summer thunderstorms happen often in Miami. So when it rains, the stadium's roof can close over the fans! In centerfield, the stadium put up a huge, colorful sculpture. It lit up and moved when a Marlins player hit a home run!

*Artist Red Grooms designed the Marlins outfield* ➤
*sculpture. It features scenes from Florida!*

# THE BASEBALL FIELD

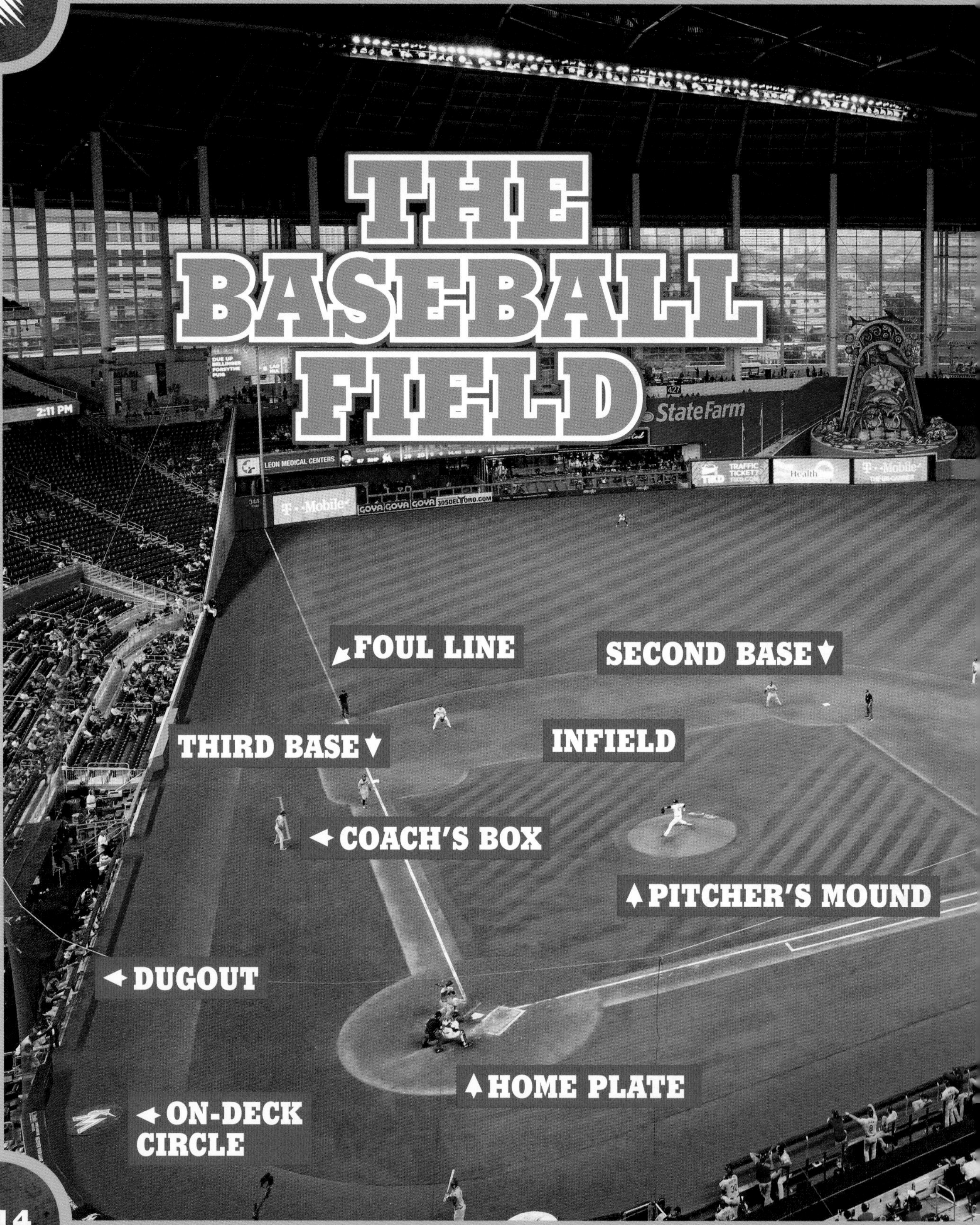

FOUL LINE ◀

SECOND BASE ▼

THIRD BASE ▼

INFIELD

◀ COACH'S BOX

▲ PITCHER'S MOUND

◀ DUGOUT

▲ HOME PLATE

◀ ON-DECK CIRCLE

OUTFIELD
FOUL LINE
FIRST BASE
OCEANBANK
pepsi
Ford
LEON MEDICAL CENTERS
K METER: 6 Ks
Fly Avianca
OCEAN BANK
DRAFTKINGS
W.B.MASON
UniVista INSURANCE
MICCOSUKEE
#MICCOSUKEELIFE
Ballpark
T-Mobile
FOX FLORIDA

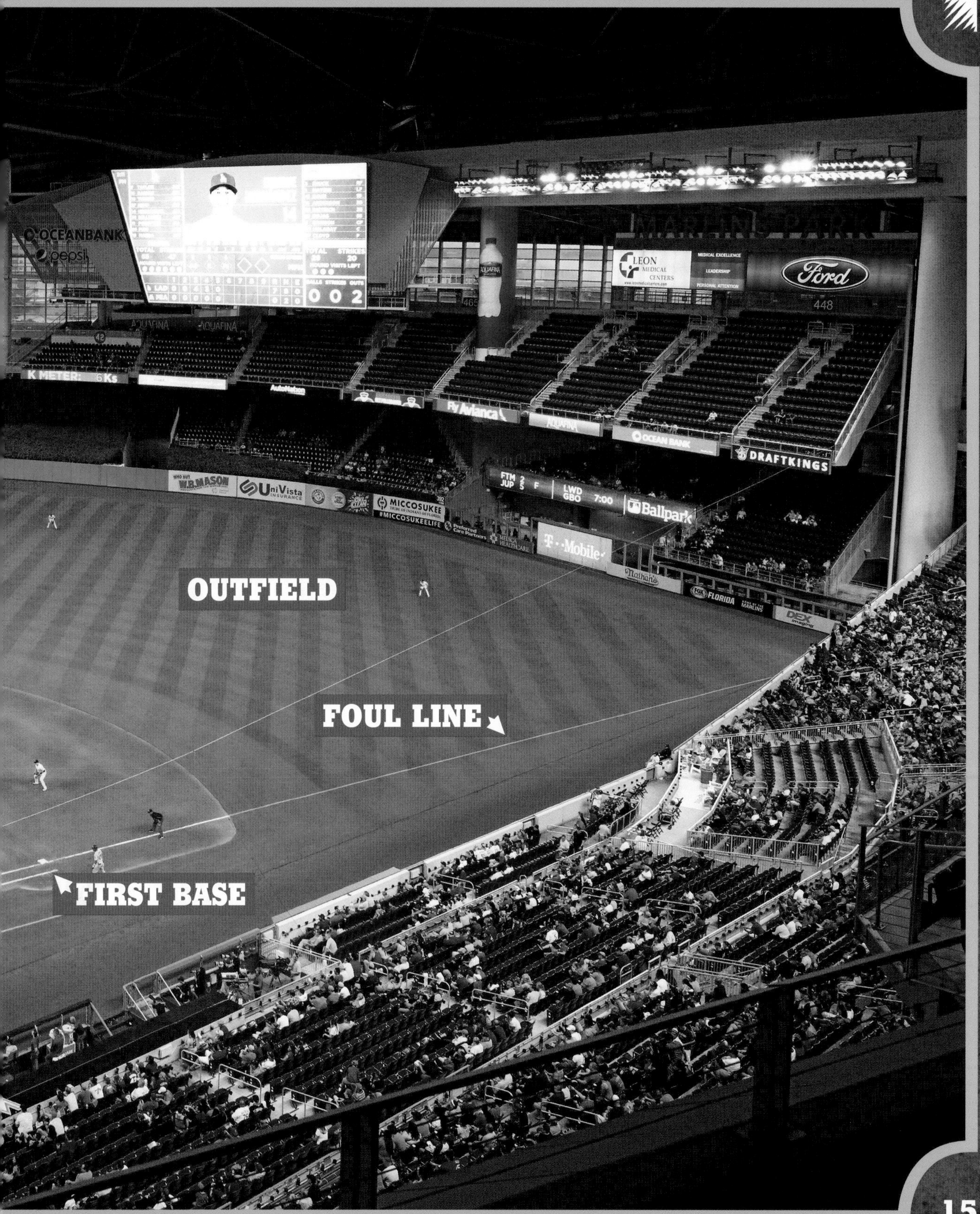

# BIG DAYS

The Marlins don't have a long history. They have had some great moments, though. Here are a few of them.

**1997**—The Marlins surprised many by winning the World Series in only their fifth season. They beat the Cleveland Indians in a seven-game thriller. Game 7 went to 11 innings!

**2003**—Florida fans watched another championship team in 2003. Led by ace pitcher Josh Beckett, the Marlins won another World Series. This time, they beat the mighty New York Yankees.

*The Marlins danced on the field after winning the 1997 World Series.* ➤

**2017**—Ichiro Suzuki played briefly for the Marlins. He left a mark. On August 1, he got his 3,054th hit. That gave him the all-time record for a player born outside the United States. Suzuki was a star in his **native** Japan before coming to MLB.

# TOUGH DAYS

Like every team, the Marlins have had some not-so-great days, too. Here are a few their fans might not want to recall.

**1998**—What a turnaround . . . in the wrong direction! A year after winning the World Series, the Marlins set a team record with 108 losses. The team had let many of its top players leave after winning the title.

**2018**—The Marlins season started out the wrong way. They lost to the Phillies 20–1. It was the worst Marlins loss ever. Pitcher Dillon Peters gave up two **grand slams**!

**2018**—Miami fans hope Derek Jeter will turn things around. In the meantime, they stayed away. The Marlins had the lowest average **attendance** of any team this season.

▼ *Dillon Peters was taken out of this 2018 game after two grand slams.*

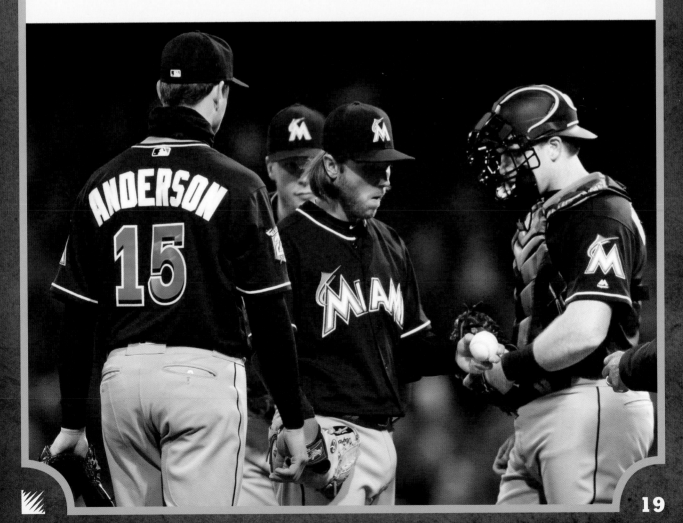

# MEET THE FANS!

**M**arlins fans have had a tough road in recent years. The last time the team had a winning record was in 2009. The future looks bright, though. New owner Derek Jeter has big plans. He wants to put a great young team together. In the meantime, fans can enjoy cheering with Billy the Marlin, the team's mascot.

◄ *Billy the Marlin's name was inspired by former New York Yankees player and manager Billy Martin.*

**L**uis Castillo starred for the Marlins for 10 seasons. He is the team's all-time leader in games, runs, and hits. Slugger Gary Sheffield was a Marlin for five seasons. He helped them win the 1997 World Series. Pitcher Josh Johnson is the team career leader in **earned run average** (ERA). He led the NL in that stat in 2010. Giancarlo Stanton had one of the best seasons ever in 2017. He was the NL MVP and hit 59 home runs. Unfortunately, he was traded to the Yankees!

*Luis Castillo led the NL in stolen bases in 2000 and 2002.* ➤

# HEROES NOW

Catcher J.T. Realmuto is one of the top players on a young Marlins team. He's a .300 hitter and a solid defensive catcher. Second baseman Starlin Castro joined the team in 2018. He could be an All-Star with his all-around talents! Jose Urena could become a key starting pitcher for Miami.

◄ *J.T. Realmuto made his first All-Star team in 2018.*

# GEARING UP

**B**aseball players wear team uniforms. On defense, they wear leather gloves to catch the ball. As batters, they wear hard helmets. This protects them from pitches. Batters hit the ball with long wood bats. Each player chooses his own size of bat. Catchers have the toughest job. They wear a lot of protection.

## THE BASEBALL

The outside of the Major League baseball is made from cow leather. Two leather pieces shaped like 8s are stitched together. There are 108 stitches of red thread. These stitches help players grip the ball. Inside, the ball has a small center of cork and rubber. Hundreds of feet of yarn are tightly wound around this center.

**CATCHER'S MASK AND HELMET** ➤

**CHEST PROTECTOR** ➤

**WRIST BANDS** ➤

**CATCHER'S MITT** ↘

## CATCHER'S GEAR

# TEAM STATS

**H**ere are some of the all-time career records for the Miami Marlins. All of these stats are through the 2018 regular season.

| HOME RUNS | |
| --- | --- |
| Giancarlo Stanton | 267 |
| Dan Uggla | 154 |

| STRIKEOUTS | |
| --- | --- |
| Ricky Nolasco | 1,001 |
| Josh Johnson | 832 |

| BATTING AVERAGE | |
| --- | --- |
| Miguel Cabrera | .313 |
| Dee Gordon | .309 |

| STOLEN BASES | |
| --- | --- |
| Luis Castillo | 281 |
| Hanley Ramirez | 230 |

| WINS | |
| --- | --- |
| Ricky Nolasco | 81 |
| Dontrelle Willis | 68 |

| SAVES | |
| --- | --- |
| Robb Nen | 109 |
| Antonio Alfonseca | 102 |

*Giancarlo Stanton thrilled Marlins fans with long homers.* ➤

| RBI | |
|---|---|
| Giancarlo Stanton | 672 |
| Mike Lowell | 578 |

# GLOSSARY

**attendance** (uh-TEND-unce) a measure of how many people are at a sporting event

**closer** (KLOH-zer) a pitcher who comes in to finish a game that his team wins

**earned run average** (URNED RUN AV-rig) a measure of how many earned runs a pitcher allows per nine innings

**expansion** (ex-PAN-shun) when something gets larger

**grand slams** (GRAND SLAMZ) home runs that happen when the bases are loaded

**native** (NAY-tiv) describing where a person was born

**rivals** (RYE-vuhls) two people or groups competing for the same thing

**World Series** (WURLD SEER-eez) the championship of Major League Baseball, played between the winners of the AL and NL

# FIND OUT MORE

## IN THE LIBRARY

Green, Tim, and Derek Jeter. *Baseball Genius*. New York: Jeter Publishing, 2018.

Jacobs, Greg. *The Everything Kids' Baseball Book, 10th Edition*. Avon, MA: Adams Media, 2016.

Sports Illustrated Kids (editors). *The Big Book of Who: Baseball*. New York, NY: Sports Illustrated Kids, 2017.

## ON THE WEB

Visit our Web site for links about the Miami Marlins: **childsworld.com/links**

*Note to Parents, Teachers, and Librarians: We routinely verify our Web links to make sure they are safe and active sites. So encourage your readers to check them out!*

# INDEX